SHELTER

SHELTER

MARTY ASHER

ARBOR HOUSE / NEW YORK

Manufactured in the United States of America

10 9 8 7 6 5 4 3 2 1
Designed by Richard Oriolo

Library of Congress Cataloging in Publication Data

Asher, Marty.
Shelter.

I. Title.
PS3551.S375S5   1986   813'.54   85-22866
ISBN: 0-87795-772-X

TO JUDY

I

This is what happened to a man named Billy in the days before the end of the world.

MARTY ASHER

He decided to write bumper stickers to warn people of the impending catastrophe. His first said:

YOU'RE ONLY GOING TO SEE THE MISSILES IN THE SKY ONCE AND THEY'RE NOT GOING TO LOOK REAL

But it took too long to read, and Billy feared it might cause accidents when he put it on his car. His next said, succinctly:

BOOM!

But that was too cold.

Billy had been married to his wife, Sara, for eighteen years. During that time, they made love together nearly every night. But now, Billy's preoccupation with universal death and destruction rendered him impotent—in spite of Sara's best efforts to arouse him which, he would be the first to admit, were awesome. As soon as Billy felt the faintest twinge of sexual desire, he would imagine the utter devastation of everything he loved and grow limp with despair.

Billy and Sarah had two sons: Wyatt, fifteen, and Jason, six. Every night, Billy would tell Jason a going-to-bed story. Jason's favorites were *Make Way for Ducklings* and *Big Joe's Trailer Truck*. Now, however, Billy questioned whether these tales were adequately preparing Jason for the sort of world he might be facing.

Wyatt spent most of his life avoiding work and practicing guitar riffs with his band, The Bugs.

One night, Billy had a dream. Charred tin cans slowly floated down from a cold, gray sky. Children picked them up and tossed them around like balls. "DON'T TOUCH THEM. IT'S THE FALLOUT!" Billy screamed. But no one heard him, and the children continued playing.

MARTY ASHER

Sara tried everything from aphrodisiacs to exotic negligees to arouse Billy, but to no avail. One night, after a dinner of curried oysters and muskmelon sherbert for dessert, Sara sauntered into the bedroom in a handpainted silk nightgown that a friend of hers had made.

"You look terrific," said Billy.

"What are you planning to do about it?" Sara asked.

"Remember."

When Billy was in college, he thought about writing novels for a living. But novels required years to write, were hard to get published, and then took ages to work their way into the cultural mainstream where they could influence people.

He considered screenplays but decided against them because of the violent stupidity of most of the films he saw.

Short stories were unsalable, and besides, nobody read them.

Bumper stickers were short, effective, and financially viable. People read them, liked them, and bought them.

At Sara's insistence, Billy consulted a nutritionist about his depleted sexual drive and depression. Dr. Wise prescribed twenty-two vitamins, minerals, amino acids, and enzymes of various colors, shapes, and sizes, which Billy dutifully took in the hope that they would provide him with extra energy and protection should he need it. Meanwhile, Billy peed blue.

Although Sara weighed a mere 100 pounds, food was the overriding passion of her life. A vegetarian since she was thirteen and saw a chicken beheaded on her aunt's farm, she now created culinary delights with eggplant, okra, and exotic vegetables and grains that Billy had never even heard of. Two years ago, she had opened her little restaurant, The Gourd, in Claverack, New York, which had gathered a faithful and growing clientele. Billy's loss of appetite disturbed her even more than his lack of interest in sex.

The Bugs had been practicing together for three years. Their song, "You, Yeah," had become a cult hit at Claverack High. As Billy worked on his bumper stickers, Wyatt snarled in the basement:

You, yeah, you think you're something,
You, yeah, you ain't nothing,
You wake up in the morning and put lipstick on your nose
  and think you're hot shit and you're making it,
Well, you ain't nowhere, you got no one,
You ain't nothing.

SHELTER

While Billy wrote, he listened to rock 'n' roll in the attic. For Billy, rock 'n' roll began and ended with the Beatles, especially their golden trilogy—*Revolver, Sgt. Pepper,* and *Abbey Road.*

Most of Billy's friends had changed with the times in their musical tastes. After outgrowing the Beatles, they graduated to the melancholy mellow of Crosby, Stills, Nash, and Young. They tripped through the heavy drug years with Procol Harum, Pink Floyd, the Moody Blues, and Jefferson Airplane. Dropping all pretense of significance, they danced through the seventies to Diana Ross and the Bee Gees, until today, they dutifully jogged, zoned from their middle-aged travails to "Beat It" pulsing through their Walkmen.

Billy, however, returned to the source daily. A side of *Revolver, Sgt. Pepper,* or *Abbey Road* began and ended his day. For variation, he would occasionally allow "Strawberry Fields," "Hey, Jude," or, when he was desperate, "All You Need Is Love." Sometimes he would reach as far ahead as "The Long and Winding Road," whose soaring violins filled him with a wistful melancholy. But with those exceptions, Billy's musical life ended in 1970 with the release of *Abbey Road.*

MARTY ASHER

Billy liked taking vitamins. Although you could feel nothing happening, you knew they were in there working, protecting you against all eventualities. As for other drugs, he utilized them far less than he did in the old days, when he was stoned more often than straight. From the bad trips of his youth, Billy knew that if you popped drugs too frequently, they made reality feel dull. The trick was to take them judiciously, Billy used to spend hours weighing the pros and cons of ingesting a particular substance before he did so. But now, after watching the news or MTV, reality required immediate distortion.

Billy first met Roland Weathers in 1968 on the roof of the graduate library at Indiana University to which Billy had adjourned for a sun bath and Roland a joint. Billy was intrigued by the spicy, pungent smoke, but declined when Roland offered him a toke, uncertain whether it was marijuana or heroin that was the addictive one.

Roland smiled.

MARTY ASHER

Roland was one of a dozen black students at Indiana—and the first to be permitted to major in Afro-American music. To Roland, this meant having the state pay his tuition, room, and board for the pleasure of spending eight hours a day stoned, listening to Miles Davis or John Coltrane, usually in bed with a newly liberated white sorority sister out to prove her worldliness. Roland's other interests included the *I Ching*, numerology, and the works of St. John of the Cross, an obscure sixteenth-century Spaniard who wrote semipornographic poems about the union of the soul with God. Roland found Billy's philosophical and poetical naiveté remarkable. Billy liked the fact that Roland gave him drugs and made him laugh a lot. They became roommates.

When Sara went off to work at four in the afternoon, Billy gave Jason his supper and bath. As he lathered Jason's fine yellow hair, he couldn't help wondering what childhood would be like followed by instant annihilation.

Weird, grim, and mercilessly incomplete.

But then again, he reasoned, would an existence spent in the pursuit of cookies and fire engines be so terrible in the larger scheme of things?

MARTY ASHER

Billy approached his bumper stickers with a zen-like peaceful-
ness of mind, much the way, he imagined, an artist approaches
a canvas. He understood the medium, appreciated its virtues,
and respected its limitations. He practiced his craft daily. Billy
believed a great bumper sticker should be simple enough to
comprehend while passing at sixty-five miles per hour. The
message should reverberate in the mind for at least ten seconds
after the first reading, then explode in the semiconsciousness in
a patina of double-entendres, i.e., I BREAK FOR VEGETABLES
(Sara's favorite). Often Billy would start with an entire para-
graph. He would slice away at the fat and contrivance until he
was left with the germ, which then had to be coddled and
refashioned to present itself in the wittiest, most memorable,
least clichéd manner. Billy tested his bumper stickers using an
amateur radar set. He would watch the rate at which people
slowed down for particular stickers, then measure how long it
took them to accelerate to their original speed. He reasoned that
the longer it took, the more effective the sticker.

Billy's first marijuana adventure was a candlelit affair replete with sweet incense, wind chimes, and Miles Davis's *Sketches of Spain*. Roland talked for an hour about the quality and genealogy of the particular herb they were going to smoke. Billy, in spite of following Roland's detailed instructions on how to inhale, insisted that he felt no effects. But when Roland asked him to turn off the light, he couldn't figure out how to slip his hand under the lamp shade to reach the switch. He touched the lamp from the top, then he sat down underneath and tried slipping his hand up, but it wouldn't reach either way.

"Strange lamp shade," said Billy.

Roland clicked the switch. "Chemistry always wins."

MARTY ASHER

Billy spent days combing bookstores and the public library for volumes about nuclear war for very young readers, but he found none. Although it had been years since he had turned his hand to a prose form as long and demanding as the story, he resolved that he would try to fashion some for Jason that might prove useful.

When Billy returned to Dr. Wise two weeks after his first appointment, she asked him if he felt any better. "Why should I?" he retorted. "Nothing's changed. Everyone is twitching for the end."

"But each of us faces death sooner or later," replied Dr. Wise.

"No," Billy said. "We're all going to die together very soon."

"I'm going to increase your dosage to 20 milligrams of B_6. I also want you to take 500 milligrams of DLPA three times a day for the depression."

"Don't *you* think the world is going to end soon?" Billy asked.

"If it does," Dr. Wise answered, "I know I'll die healthy."

Billy sold his first group of bumper stickers to a local gift shop. He was surprised and delighted when they reordered. Soon Billy's bumper stickers appeared in stores throughout the Hudson Valley. His first group was:

CHILDREN HAVE SUCH LITTLE NOSES

HAVE A NICE DAY BUT DON'T BE TOO PUSHY ABOUT IT

and

THIS BUMPER STICKER HAS NO OTHER PURPOSE THAN TO GET YOU TO READ IT

After they had successfully navigated the lamp crisis, Roland grabbed Billy and walked him down the stairs. Billy became transfixed by the paisley pattern on the carpeting, which kept luring him back up.

"We can't disobey the rug, man," he laughed hysterically.

"Come on, soldier," said Roland. "The foxhole's just around the bend."

They ended up at a high school masquerade dance. Billy sat in a corner, gawking at Superman dancing with a two-peopled horse. After Roland took the phone number of the rear section of the horse, they went back to his apartment and had a pack of Chips Ahoy! and a quart of milk each.

"Pebbles and waterfalls," Billy mused.

"Just what the world needs," said Roland, "another stoned poet."

MARTY ASHER

One night in bed, after much groping and wrestling, Sara pleaded with Billy. "If it's the end of the world, don't you think we should grasp every moment and make the most of it, as if it might be our last?"

"No," said Billy. "We should grasp every moment and do something to ensure that it isn't."

"But what can one person do?" Sara asked.

"I'm working on it."

Roland had met Sara in Bloomington, Indiana, at the local natural foods restaurant where she worked as a part-time waitress. One day over lunch, he introduced her to Billy, who fell in love with her as soon as she said, "They're pushing the zucchini, but I'd stick with the eggplant." Billy had seen Sara on campus many times and admired her long red hair which cascaded down to her tiny waist. She invited him to her apartment that night, casually removed her clothes, and said, "Don't you want to make love to me?" Billy, still a virgin, nervously replied, "When do you need to know?"

MARTY ASHER

In spite of Sara's objections, Billy felt it was his obligation as a father to inform Jason, as best he could, about what might occur.

THE GREAT FIRE

Once there was a three-story building in a large city. One day the first floor caught fire. A little boy named Raphael called the fire department. Quickly, the screaming engines arrived, and the firemen put out the fire with their big hoses. The next day the first and second floors caught fire. Once again, Raphael called the fire department, and once again they put out the fire. The next day the whole building caught fire. Raphael called the fire department as he had done before. He waited and waited, but no fire engines came, and the building burned to the ground.

What happened?" Jason asked.
"Beats me," said Billy.

SHELTER

While marijuana remained Billy's favorite everyday reality improver, there was no denying the therapeutic benefits of occasional doses of LSD, alcohol, Valium, and most infrequently, cocaine, when they were used for rare special occasions. Speed, however, always left him cold. Things seemed to be moving quickly enough of their own accord.

Billy kept his pharmaceuticals in a gray metal storage box in the attic. When the missiles came, it would be the first and last thing he'd grab.

To relax Billy before the first time they made love, Sara rubbed him from top to toe with her homemade cucumber-scented cream.

Afterward, Billy grinned at her sheepishly. "It didn't hurt," he said.

While Jason tried to integrate Billy's apocalyptic visions into his little world, Wyatt had long since rejected all adult values, especially ones as useless as his father's. Wyatt assumed that sooner or later it would all blow, but that was no reason not to try to look your best and become a rock 'n' roll star if you could.

Billy placed ads in the classified sections of *Mother Jones* and *The New York Review of Books.* The first list was a mixed success:

MAD POETS DO IT WITHOUT RHYME
OR REASON   1,197 sold

HONK FOR HONK'S SAKE   564 sold

PRONOUNS ARE THE KEY TO
ANONYMITY   12 sold

Billy, Sara, and Roland moved in together. Billy now looked back on this period fondly as one of his happiest times. The three of them would smoke, ride around the countryside in Sara's orange VW, and go skinny dipping in the quarries. They spent long summer evenings on the porch devouring some of Sara's more and less successful experiments: an incredible curried barley, mushroom, lentil, and carrot loaf; an insipid soybean and cucumber tart; and lemon frosties, which Sarah materialized from lemons, honey, water, and magic. Afterward, in a pleasant grass-wine stupor, they listened to Miles or Coltrane. Sara and Billy would then retire to lengthy, languorous sessions of stoned love-making. Roland would ease down to Sorority Row where he would try to fulfill his goal of fucking every blonde sociology major at the university before Christmas.

Jason started to collect fire engines. Large red plastic ones. Small natural wooden ones. Antique fire engines. Remote control fire engines. Fire engine hats. Fire engine records. An encyclopedia of fire engines that gave the gallons-per-second pumping capacity of all operating pumper tankers. Jason spent most of his waking hours maneuvering his fire engines into different patterns. When the great fire came, he would be ready.

Before Sara brought home *Revolver*, Billy had heard the Beatles' music many times, and while he appreciated its liveliness and clean sound, he did not find it particularly special. But three joints and a hearing of *Revolver* were a revelation. While Roland droned on about how the Beatles had stolen this technique from African music and that one from jazz, to Billy the effect was staggering. "Eleanor Rigby" made him cry in its touching evocation of loneliness. "Got to Get You into My Life" and "Good Day Sunshine" tickled him with their unexpected chord changes and syncopations. When he was sad, *Revolver* made him happy. When he was manic, it soothed him. If he was perplexed, the music said, "Don't worry; it's not that important."

Having played the clarinet since he was eight, Billy started out as a classical music major at college. Like many of his fellow students at the time, he quickly came to second guess his earlier decision. In fact, the very notion of having to choose a career, of having to make a commitment now for the rest of his life, seemed like an antiquated warp in the social structure rather than something to take seriously. He switched to comparative literature, then to creative writing, taking courses along the way in Chinese, philosophy, and economics. The combination of skills he acquired coincidentally helped prepare him for his life's work. The music training improved the sound and cadence of his stickers. The writing and philosophy aided the style and substance. The Chinese eliminated some of his Western biases. And the economics aided the management of the company.

Billy's first successful nuclear bumper sticker was:

ROCK 'N' ROLL IS HERE TO STAY BUT ONLY IF WE
ARE

As the result of an ad in *Rolling Stone,* it sold over 5,000 copies
and became Billy's biggest hit.

MARTY ASHER

Much to Sara's dismay, Billy continued his program of Jason's nuclear education with stories like:

THE MAGIC LIGHTS

Once upon a time there was a boy named Avril who lived on a mountain. Every morning he would wake up and see the sun rising, and every evening he would go to bed and see the sun setting. Some nights he would see the moon as well. One day while he was eating lunch, his father said, "Avril, how would you like to see some special extra-bright lunchtime lights as well?"

Avril said, "No thanks."

The next day, Avril woke to see the sun rising, and when he went to bed, he saw the sun setting, and later, the moon rising. That afternoon, Avril's father again said, "Are you sure you wouldn't like to see some special, extra-bright lunchtime lights as well?"

Avril again said, "No thanks."

The day after, at four o'clock in the morning, Avril's father woke him and said, "It's time for lunch." And he ate the most delicious lunch he ever had—peanut butter sandwiches, hamburgers, potato chips, and all the cakes and cookies and ice cream he wanted. After he finished, neither Avril nor his father were ever seen or heard from again.

"What do you think happened to them?" asked Billy.
"Maybe they ate too much," said Jason.

Billy and Roland took LSD, with Sara lying across their madras bedspread, reading from the Tibetan Book of the Dead. Billy had so many profound revelations that he could hardly write them down fast enough in his notebook:

Everything that ever was or is or will be either was or is or will be.

Some cars have happy faces (Toyotas, Saabs, Volvos), and others have mean ones (Chryslers, Mercedes). The Mercury Cougar is perplexed.

If we don't actually see the flowers growing, it's just because we're not looking carefully enough.

Everybody's weird.

MARTY ASHER

Billy's bumper stickers continued to thrive, although they began to take on a more sinister disposition. His next group read:

ROCK-IT NOT ROCKETS

NUCLEAR = UNCLEAR

and

TODAY MAY BE THE LAST DAY OF THE REST OF
  YOUR LIFE

One night, at three in the morning, while plugged into his Walkman listening to "Within You Without You," Billy sat bolt upright in bed, terrified. He suddenly realized that not only were people in danger of instant extinction, but music was as well. And the thought of a world without the beauty, energy, and humor of the Beatles' music hurt him almost as much as the destruction of humanity.

MARTY ASHER

Billy and Sara got married in a ceremony held in front of the graduate library, attended by a half dozen teachers and students. Afterward, they planned to move back east. Roland decided he had had enough of the midwest and it was time to return to San Francisco. Roland, Billy, and Sara all embraced after the wedding and promised to write. "You won't, but I will," said Roland.

One afternoon Billy showed up at The Gourd quite stoned.
While he waited for Sara, he doodled on some of the menus,
then put them back when she arrived.

APPETIZERS

Stuffed Mushrooms
(Mushrooms stuffed with succulent
bits of cheese, vegetables, butter, bread crumbs,
and herbs)

Asparagus Vinaigrette

Curried Eggplant

ATTENTION MR. OR MS. CONSUMER. VEGETABLES ARE SWELL
AND IT'S LOVELY TO SIT HERE STUFFING OUR ORGANIC
FACES WITH THEM AND THINKING WE'RE BUDDHA CAUSE
WE'RE NOT MURDERING COWS BUT I'M NOT TALKING ABOUT
COW MURDER ALTHOUGH NUCLEAR WAR IS NOT GOING TO
BE VERY GOOD FOR COWS EITHER OR EVEN FOR
EGGPLANTS. WHY DON'T YOU THINK ABOUT WHAT YOU PLAN
TO DO ABOUT IT BEFORE STARTING YOUR NEXT COURSE? WE
NOW RETURN YOU TO YOUR FOOD.

MARTY ASHER

Afterward, Sara said, "I'm worried about you, Billy."

"So am I," Billy replied.

"When does this all end?"

"When it ends."

"What's it supposed to accomplish?"

"I'm not sure."

"You're no fun anymore."

"Fun," Billy repeated. "Fun is the one thing that money can't buy."

When Billy returned to Dr. Wise for his fifth visit and still reported no difference in his appetite or libido, she increased his dosage of B_6 tenfold. "There may be a side effect," she warned. "You may hallucinate."

"How can I tell?" Billy asked.

In spite of Dr. Wise's orders, Billy began to smoke grass again and even managed to score some LSD from Wyatt's high school. His profits, meanwhile, plummeted on the basis of losers like:

WHY ARE YOU READING THIS STUPID BUMPER STICKER WHEN YOU SHOULD BE PUTTING YOUR AFFAIRS IN ORDER?

WE DESERVE WHAT WE GET

WHAT A WASTE OF TALENT

HAVE DESSERT. IT DOESN'T MATTER

SHELTER

Billy wondered whether his obsession with the Beatles was just nostalgia for a time when life was simpler. Was there really a power in this music to move and fundamentally change the world, or was this just an adolescent delusion? Did his parents feel the same way about Harry James? Would Jason feel the same way about Michael Jackson? Was it all merely a hallucination? If so, why was he the only one still hallucinating? Where were the other millions? Just going about their daily lives waiting for the bomb to hit them on the head? What had happened? What had gone wrong? Maybe the only way to find out was to go back to the music. If the power was ever there, it should still be there. Maybe no one was listening right.

Dear Billy,
Even in these peculiar times it is customs, alas, that our lives
are built upon, though how many lives are built on anything
these days? In my thirtieth year, however, I know better than all
you horny diaper dudes, so I take your silence with the mere
thoughtlessness with which it is given and do not impute it to
mean anything malicious like you don't love me anymore,
which, we all know, is impossible. Your message for the year:
Maturity is having the same thing happen to you a lot. Be kind
to Sara. Women who will put up with the likes of you are rare.

Fondly,
Roland

Mon Guillaume:

Those of us not blessed or cursed with the creative juices of
tigers like yourself must content ourselves to be the glue that
holds together other and greater lives, and, as I have told you,
the stars, the numbers, and my everloving black soul tell me
that greater things are in store for you. Therefore, I continue to
make it easy for you with this business-reply friendship that
requires nothing more than your opening an envelope once a
year, which, I assume, even a lazy, self-indulgent motherfucker
like you can handle. Joys of the season.

R.

William:
What's this? An actual *response*. Will wonders never cease? A father. How original. Proceed. Peace.

R.

P. S. Of course I'll be godfather. Every red-blooded American white boy should have a stoned, black, alternative daddy on the coast.

Billiboy:

At this point in my calculations you are about to enter into a significant phase, which may explain your stony silence. Either that, or you've smoked your brains out to the point where you can no longer lift a pen. Nevertheless, your faithful friend takes a moment of repose from his New Year's orgy to wish you, as ever, the very finest of years, though you don't deserve it. But mine is a forgiving race.

R.

January 1973

My dear William:
Since you are still wet behind the proverbial ears, if indeed they
are still functioning after listening to the garbage you call
music, I once again find it in my heart to forgive, but not to
forget. Alas, since we are on the verge of four more years of
Richard Nixon as our leader (*and are still alive!!!!*), we kindred
spirits should certainly keep in touch to guard our feeble
strength. May the good Lord keep you since no one else will.

Roland

BILLY,
NOT WANTING TO SEEM LIKE YOUR MOTHER, STILL
A REPLY WOULD BE NICE IF ONLY TO CONFIRM
THAT YOU ARE ALIVE AND LIVING AT THE SAME
ADDRESS. SHOULD AULD ACQUAINTANCE—

ROLAND

MARTY ASHER

June 1974

Dear William:
Did I wish you a Happy New Year this year? If not, Happy New
Year. If so, did my wishing work? Not that I claim responsibility
for your happiness. But don't cross me just to play safe.
  Will the 70s ever end?

R.

SHELTER

January 1975

Billiam:
Don't mean to crowd you with a double dose within a calendar
year. Ignore last missive. Weirdtime at the hacienda. Juanita
has gone back south of the border and Inge keeps me cool.
Happies to your tribe.

Roland

Bile:

Analogies between my life and song "California Girls" extremely unkind, especially when *Pet Sounds* was *your* fave, as I recall, before the Brits converted you. Anyway, Inge split and I'm going back to God. At least she's faithful. Enjoy the buy-centennial.

R.

Dear Billy,
Stoned and alone. Just me and Miles listening to the new year
spin in. Thanks for the bumper stickers. Please send a car.

R.

Darling Billy:

Nixon goes. The Beatles go. But we continue. Has it ever occurred to you that the only reason I keep this relationship going is to drum up business for the Post Office, which looks like it might be following the railroads down the tubes? Of course not. That's why I love you.

Uncle Rollikins

January 1979

Dear B,
In love and in Mexico.

R.

Dear Billy and Sara,
Spending Christmas with you was as comforting as watching a
television coffee advertisement. Living in San Francisco one
occasionally deludes oneself into thinking this is real life. Wyatt
reminds me of you, Billy. Shows promise but requires season-
ing. I don't care if he likes it and it makes him sleep. Remove
all Kiss records from the house immediately. This is serious.

R.

January 1981

Dear Daddy,
Another child. God, what fertile creatures you are. Congratulations to the bearer of the good news. And in this decade of sequels, how could I not be honored to be Godfather II?

R.

January 1982

Dear William:
So now you're becoming rich and famous. How do you always
manage to do what you're supposed to be doing while I just do
what I've always been doing? Why do you ma-ture and I de-
tour? The name of the place is I Like It Like That.

R.

Billy!

An abominable year. A social disease and a grass drought make me impossible to live with. Man the whole fucking peninsula is heading for the hills. Even the hills are splitting. That's why we're having all these earthquakes. I mean if you can't get laid and you can't get stoned, what's left? Television? God? Nirvana? Definitely not my style. But what do you care, curling up with your beaujolays while I can't even make it with a bored doe. But from my bed of agony I wish you all the best.

Rolled-in

Dear William:

I figure the end is near. The Post Office just promoted me to floor foreman. Something about equal opportunity. They're whipping out the champagne in Acapulco and Thailand. Surely the end is near.

R.

Dear Billy:

Your cards and letters and pictures help but turning 40 stings nevertheless. I went out with Carmen to prove that I could still party. I can still party, but the next day seems to dawn about 12 hours earlier than it used to. I feel the calling of mortality. Wouldn't you think mortality would have better to do than go for the likes of me? But mortality is a democrat, so here I am, 40 and fucked. But I won't mature. I swear it.

Rocking Horse R.

Dear Bill,
I am now night shift manager of the whole fucking Embarcadero Branch of the San Francisco Post Office. Land of opportunity! Land of the Pilgrims' Pride. Head for the fucking phones man. Gonna be party time at the old P.O.

Commander Stamplicker

Sometimes Billy wondered why Wyatt and his friends, who had a much larger stake in the continuity of things than he did, didn't protest their death sentence. Certainly, millions of 15-year-olds refusing to go to school until peace talks were held would be an effective bargaining chip. But Wyatt seemed uninterested.

Once Billy suggested that he organize a protest among his classmates.

Wyatt said, "No one gives a shit about that stuff."

"Why?" Billy pursued it.

"Because it's ugly, stupid, and boring."

"But what if you all die from an ugly and stupid and boring bomb?"

"Can I go now?" Wyatt replied.

Little fortunes started appearing in Sara's legendary fudge
brownie cookies:

THE END IS NOT NEAR—IT'S HERE

THIS IS THE WAY THE WORLD ENDS—NOT WITH A
   BANG, BUT A CRUMBLE

IF YOU DON'T WANT YOUR COOKIES
   RADIOACTIVE, THEN WHY ARE YOU SO
   GODDAMN PASSIVE?

Sara told Billy to stay away from the restaurant.

Billy spent all his time now in the attic listening to music and waiting for the end. He occasionally came down for meals, but then he just stared into space and rarely ate anything.

Aren't you hungry?" Jason asked one time.

"Starved."

"Then why don't you eat?"

"I'm practicing."

Even Wyatt, usually oblivious to everything outside his music, became concerned. "If you die," he said one night after Billy hadn't eaten again, "who'll pay for my guitar lessons?"

"Even nuclear annihilation has its bright side," Billy replied.

"I don't think all this is good for Jason and Wyatt," Sara said to Billy when they were in bed.

"Really? I would have appreciated it if someone had prepared me, but I suppose mothers know best."

"Billy, I'm leaving."

"Where will you go?"

"I've rented a small apartment near the restaurant."

"And the children?"

"They'll come with me. You can see them whenever you like, only no more stories."

"When will you come back?"

"When *you* come back, even if it takes a hundred years."

"No," said Billy. "If we survive the next two or three, it should be all downhill after that."

The next day Sara packed three suitcases of clothes and left. The day after, a moving van removed all the furniture except for the stereo, which Billy had owned before he met Sara. Living in the empty house without Sara and the children to anchor him, Billy grew even more despondent. He ate sporadically, and when the food in the house was finished, he just drank wine. He never washed, shaved, or changed his clothes. He lived in the attic, listening to *Sgt. Pepper*. He played it at 33, at 45, and at 78 RPMs. He spun it backward by hand to see if there was anything he had missed. He bought the digital master and listened to that. He listened to it stoned. He listened to it straight. Incredibly enough, no matter how often he played it, this record seemed to be the only thing left on earth that still had the power to amaze him.

In a fit of hopelessness, Billy ran to his pharmaceutical box—his psychic fallout shelter in case the end came. He stared at the herbs, pills, and powders with the sense of having rediscovered a long lost friend. No ordinary stoning would do tonight. Something major was in order. Start with a few sticks of sensimilla to get things going. A couple of hits of Roland's Christmas coke to give it an edge. A few 'ludes to keep it from getting out of hand. A bottle of Kenwood Cabernet Sauvignon for the spirit and a handful of Dr. Wise's vitamins for the body. And off we go. The two tabs of LSD Billy had snuggled safely in their tissue paper nest were reserved for the final track.

MARTY ASHER

Ten minutes or an hour later, it grew dark. The audience squirmed in their seats. Then the show began, and Billy knew that everything would turn out all right, as it always had. Only this time, halfway through "Being For the Benefit of Mr. Kite," he looked up and saw a figure sitting on the window sill, and there was no mistaking it, from the bright green satin uniform with red piping to the wire-rimmed glasses to the gentle sneer. John had come.

"You're alive," Billy said.

"For you, I'm alive. Why do you want me here?"

" 'Cause I love you and I miss you and I'm scared and I don't know what to do. It's all been downhill since you left and the world is a disaster and I can't handle it anymore. I don't want to space out like everyone else and pretend that it's just not happening. I want you to tell me what to do. Get people on the track again. Make it like it was."

"No problem," said John, pulling out a joint from behind his ear and offering Billy a toke. "Sure I can do that. But you've got to help. I mean I'm fucking dead, man. That stupid fucker fucking *killed* me, and I was writing my best stuff. I was in a whole other place."

"So what happens now?"

"I'm not sure. I can't see into the future or anything like that. I have a hard time focusing. But I'll tell you one thing. It's all in the music."

"I know that," said Billy.

But the side ended.

Billy got up, navigated his way across the debris strewn floor to the stereo, turned the record over, and lit another joint.

"I mean have you ever listened to it? *Really?*" John continued. "You'd be amazed by some of the shit we put into those tracks. People still haven't found it yet." He passed him the joint.

"I'm listening now," Billy pointed out, while "Within You Without You" continued to play.

"No. I mean *really* listened," said John. You've got to keep playing every track until you get it."

"Get what?"

"Get back to where you once belonged," John laughed.

"Okay," Billy exhaled. "I'll listen."

"You'd better hurry."

"Why?"

"There's not a lot of time. When we were cutting the record, our Indian guru told us it would live as long as mankind lived, but twenty years from now no one would remember it. Next year is the twentieth anniversary of *Sgt. Pepper.*"

"Holy shit," said Billy.

With the final, endless chord of "A Day in the Life," John was gone.

Billy ran down to Sara's new apartment, banged on her door till she woke up, and said, "I need to borrow 500 dollars."

"Why?" Sara asked.

"If I tell you," said Billy, "you won't give it to me."

"Try me."

"Because the future of mankind is at stake."

"Then mankind may be doomed. I only have about 200 dollars."

"That'll save North America," said Billy.

Jason was thrashing around in his bed. The kid had never been a peaceful sleeper. Billy kissed him on the cheek and he was instantly awake. "I've got to split for a while," Billy said. "I've got some work to do in California."

"Where's California?"

"Very far away."

"Do they have fire engines there?"

"Lots."

"Will you send me some?"

"Assuming they're not all in use."

Wyatt was staring at the ceiling listening to The Police through his Walkman when he saw Billy's shadow above his head.

"I'm going for a while."

"Bye."

"Don't you want to know where?"

"Uh, where?"

"California," said Billy. "I'm going to stay there with Roland till things settle in."

"That's cool."

"If it all blows before I get back and you're still alive, take care of everybody."

"No problem," said Wyatt.

"Roland?"

"Shit, you motherfucker, what time is it?"

"I don't know, but this is important. I have to do it. If I don't, no one else will."

"Do what?"

"Save the world."

"Uh huh."

"I have a plan."

"You're not the white one for nothing."

"I have to go back and find out what went wrong. Nobody's ever analyzed the music right so we can see what was there and how we blew it."

"You mean Miles?"

"Not Miles, Roland. We're not into *The Great African Nation* trip right now. We're talking about saving civilization."

"Only one kind of music powerful enough for that."

"You better believe it."

"White man music."

"Hey, I can't help it."

"White man music made by four Englishmen who got rich, found truth, and either got shot or are singing with Michael Jackson or playing parts in TV miniseries."

"This isn't a joke, Roland. I just saw John. He was sitting here in my fucking bedroom, man. And you know what he says? He says it's all in the music."

"Heavy."

"One other thing. Sara's left me. She thinks I'm getting too weird for the kids."

"I can't imagine why."

"I want to come visit you. I want to do this work in San Francisco."

"Hey little honkey, I'm rollin' as we speak."

II

The stewardess tapped him on the shoulder and signaled for him to remove his headphones. "Sir," she said in a midwestern drawl, "you're disturbing this lady sitting next to you. Do you think you could keep your voice down?"

"ASSHOLE!" Billy screamed.

"Santa Maria," said the woman.

"It all starts out of chaos," Billy whispered into his portable tape recorder as the first track of *Sgt. Pepper's Lonely Hearts Club Band* boomed into the head phones of his Walkman. The old woman with the plaid shawl drew closer to the window. Billy flashed a peace sign at her and went back to work.

"It sounds like a symphony," he continued, "a rock 'n' roll symphony. Like one by Beethoven. Beethoven was the one who was deaf, wasn't he? They're telling us we're all deaf." Billy fast-forwarded ahead to "A Little Help from My Friends." *Lend me your ears and I'll sing you a song.* "Yes, of course," he said. "Don't worry, John. I hear you. It took twenty years, but I hear you."

Twenty years. . . . Billy reversed back to the beginning of the tape. *It was twenty years ago today.* Jesus, John wasn't shittin'. Twenty years.

The woman signaled the stewardess and mumbled something to her as John sang about Billy Shears. Shears, Billy thought . . . the cutting edge. "AND MY FUCKING NAME'S BILLY," he screamed. "It's all in the goddamn music!"

"Sir," said the stewardess, "you'll really have to keep it down."

MARTY ASHER

It was five years since Billy had seen Roland. He had stayed in Claverack for a week. The three of them had reminisced about old times and why everything had not turned out the way they thought it would. Billy confessed that he thought by this time money, poverty, weapons, and virtually all evil greater than shoplifting would have disappeared.

"Jesus Christ," Roland had responded. "You went to all those rallies 'cause you actually believed in all that stuff."

"Why did you go?" Billy asked.

"Sex and drugs, white boy, sex and drugs."

Billy wrote:

Dear Sara,
Obviously we're in two different places now. You're eggplant as usual, and I'm waiting for the bombs to fall. Until one of us is proven right (hopefully, though not probably, you), it ain't gonna work. Therefore:
1) I'm going to California to see Roland for a while.
2) I figure if it all ain't over by the time I get back then you're right and I'm wrong, and if you can handle it, we can try again.
3) If I'm right and you're wrong, it don't matter none.
4) You know I love you.

Maybe it'll all work out.

B.

P.S. I think I'm on the verge of something major.
P.P.S. Thanks for the bucks. I'll pay you back if there's still money.

MARTY ASHER

Billy ordered two brandies. He was still flying a little from the drug marathon the night before, but the woman sitting next to him had disturbed him and he had to get back into the spirit again. His one remaining joint nestled snugly in his shirt pocket in case of an emergency. He assumed Roland would be waiting with reinforcements when he arrived. He pushed "Play."

"No . . . no . . . don't worry, Ringo, I'm not going to walk out on you. No, that's all over. Oh my God." *What do you do at the end of the day? Does it worry you to be alone?* "They know about Sara. They fucking know Sara's split!"

"Sorry," Billy said to the woman who had looked up from her copy of *Woman's Day.*

Get high with a little help from my friends. "Roland. Of course. Jesus. It's really all here."

Wyatt had graced Roland with a performance of his latest composition, "It Don't Mean Nothin',"

> *You think it means somethin' when you say you got*
>   *money—wrong, it don't mean nothin';*
> *You think I'm gonna bag myself when you say you ain't my*
>   *honey—wrong, it don't mean nothin';*
> *Nothin' ain't worth nothin' if you don't want somethin', and*
>   *I don't want nothin' so who cares? Who cares?*
> *You think you're a madonna cause you're smokin' marijuana*
>   *but it don't mean nothin'—nothin' at all. Have a ball.*

"Amazing," Roland had responded, "how talent runs so thick in one family. Most notable transmission of genes since Andrew Jackson begat Jessie and Michael."

Dear Jason,

I'm on my way to make sure the hoses on all the fire engines are ready for The Great Fire because I think it's coming soon. You take care of your mom and listen to whatever she says. I'm sorry if my stories have been scaring you. You'll understand why I have been telling them to you when you get older, assuming you have the opportunity.

Your loving father

Billy went off to the john and stared at himself in the mirror. His hair was filthy and matted. The red ribbon he had used to tie it back dangled from one ear and hung over his chest. He had spilled wine over the front of his white Indian cotton shirt, and it looked like a purple wound. He sniffed around and realized that he stank. He took off his shirt and washed his face and chest, scrubbing vigorously under the arms.

No wonder that old lady was freaked out, he thought. He filled the basin with warm water, stooped down, stuck the front half of his head in, then turned around and got the back. He soaped it up, rinsed the same way, then filled the basin up with cold water and rinsed again. He squeezed his hair dry, re-tied the ribbon, stuck his shirt under his arm, and emerged from the bathroom, brushing past a sullen, acne-speckled fourteen-year-old with a giant crucifix dangling from one ear, who regarded him with awe.

"You take drugs," Billy winked as he walked by, "and this is what happens."

MARTY ASHER

The night before Roland left New York, the three of them went to The Joyous Lake in Woodstock, where some esoteric sixties groups who had never made it very big performed their stuff to an appreciative, suitably hirsuted and attired audience. They had smoked some of Roland's finest herb, eaten and drunk themselves stupid, and listened to about twenty minutes of music when Billy abruptly got up and walked out.

Roland and Sara charged after him. "What's wrong?" Roland asked.

"This reminds me of those late night TV ads. All the sixties hits you can buy for six dollars and ninety-nine cents plus postage. Makes me feel like a fucking antique."

They went to a coffee shop across the street.

"They all look so fat, rich, and tired," said Billy.

"They're doin' the best they can," said Sara.

"You guys thrash it out," said Roland. "I'm goin' back for the waitress."

He returned to his seat, barechested, reached up to the overhead rack and dumped the contents of his suitcase on the seat: a few shirts, another pair of jeans, six bottles of vitamins, his Beatles tapes, and four packs of Chips Ahoy! he had picked up in the supermarket as a present for Roland. He stuffed a few in his mouth, then offered them to his seatmate, who just shook her head. He selected a blue T-shirt that showed an oval Aztec sculpture on one side and said SUNSHINE COMPANY on the back.

He crammed everything into the suitcase and started to put it back, smiling at the old lady all the time. "Oops," he said, "forgot something." He opened the suitcase, reached into the pocket of the shirt he had been wearing, removed the joint and stuck it behind his ear.

"Just Gauloise," he whispered to the woman as he sat down.

Back to work. "Lucy in the sky with diamonds," he softly harmonized. "Got to be the greatest song in the history of the world. But what does it mean? What the fuck does it mean?" He listened to the three thuds that preceded the chorus, banging his arm on the armrest. Lucy . . . he thought. Lucy . . . Lucid in the sky. They know I'm on a plane and I've gotten it. Diamonds. Truth. Eternal values and all that shit. I'm coming close. "Thanks, John, I needed that," he whispered and slumped back in his seat as the stewardess lowered his tray and deposited dinner in front of him. The tape shouted, *IT'S GETTING BETTER ALL THE TIME.*

"Amen," said Billy. He pushed "Stop" and sat up to eat.

"You come this way often?" Billy asked as he poured the remaining contents of his second brandy into his coffee.

"No," said the woman and then went back to her chicken.

"Sorry if I got a little carried away there before," he continued. "I'm working on this project and I just got excited."

"That's no problem," she said. "Just let me sleep. I have a long trip."

"Where you goin'?"

"Sacramento."

"What's there?"

"I have a new grandson," she said, smiling.

"Far out," said Billy. "I've got two kids. Both boys. I miss them a lot, but I've got this secret project I've got to do out in San Francisco. National security and all that."

"You CIA?" she asked.

"Not exactly," said Billy.

"Good. I don't like those people. They're sneaky. That's not the way this country should be."

"I know. That's why I'm going out to California. To try to make it better. . . . for your little grandson. What's his name?"

"Christopher," said the woman.

"For little Christopher," said Billy, smiling.

"Finish your chicken and let me sleep," said the woman.

Billy took out his pad again:

Dear Wyatt,
I know responsibility isn't cool, but try not to be too weird
while I take care of business out here. If I get good reports,
I'll consider letting you wear an earring when I return.

Dad

The cabin darkened as the movie began. Superman III or IV or V. He didn't have a headset (hell, he had his own), but he enjoyed watching the caped wonder crashing down buildings, picking up cars, saving children. "Right on, man," he whispered. "I wish we had a superman, but we don't, so I guess I'm stuck with me." Fuckin' world. He switched on "Fixing a Hole." "Yeah, John," he muttered as he slid down into his seat. "I do believe my mind is wandering. . . ."

Billy was standing in the doorway waving to Sara, who wore her dressing gown, and to Jason and Wyatt, still in pajamas, as the lush sound of a string orchestra welled up behind them. Billy walked away, tears in his eyes. The sky was bright orange as the sun rose. Over in the distance, Billy saw a kite. He started running toward it, leaped up, and then he was flying. The Golden Gate bridge flashed foward at mind-crackling speed. He flew past it, hundreds of red ribbons waving wildly from his back. His superhearing picked up the cheers of the people as they stopped their cars to watch. "LOOK . . . UP IN THE SKY . . . IT'S A BIRD . . . IT'S A PLANE . . . IT'S SUPER-FREAK!" A casual wave to the crowds, then on to Livermore Laboratories.

Dr. Death saw him coming through the window. "Just as I planned, my little doomed drop-out," he cackled. From the black kite above the lab, the greed ray burned through Billy just as he flew in through the window. Billy felt it pulsing in his brain. *Ferraris . . . Linda Ronstadt . . . the best Acapulco grass money can buy . . . the original masters of all the Beatles records . . . they're all yours . . . just leave me here to do my work.*

Billy stood on the window sill outside the lab. He looked down at the crowd. He saw Wyatt and Jason below, waving.

"Oh my God!" a voice cried out from the crowd. "He's got the baby!" Dr. Death had climbed out on the adjoining window ledge, and the baby dangled perilously from the tape of his disposable diaper. "My Christopher!" the lady shouted. "You must save my Christopher!"

"You make one move and the kid's a quiche," snarled Dr. Death. Faster then the speed of light, Billy flew down to Mexico to the best marijuana fields he knew. He returned before anyone had blinked and lit up a twenty-foot-long joint. With his superbreath he blew it directly at Dr. Death, who looked up at Billy, looked down at the baby, hesitated a moment, then said, "God. I'm starving." A quickie, speed-of-light trip to the Safeway ("Please let me go ahead of you. I only have one item."), and Dr. Death stared at a six-foot-high pile of Chips Ahoys! He jumped back in the room, put the baby on the floor, and greedily lunged for the cookies.

Billy grabbed the baby and watched as Dr. Death stuffed the cookies into his ever-widening mouth. Suddenly he was no longer Dr. Death, but a horse. He somersaulted out the window and, with the sound of thunder, burst into a gigantic mushroom-shaped cloud of joints and Chips Ahoys! and Linda Ronstadt records and Maseratis that slowly sailed to the earth below as the cheering crowd scrambled for the toys of their dreams.

Billy took a cab to Roland's house. The driver told Billy that he drove six months of the year in order to support his studies in India for the rest. "All the holy men say that the end of the age of reason is coming," he reported. "The age of faith is about to begin—after the age of fire."

"Age of fire," Billy repeated.

MARTY ASHER

Roland was sitting on the stoop. He ran to the cab, threw his arms around Billy, and laughed his loud, infectious cackle. He looked a little older and thinner, had lost all his hair, and his scalp shone almost as brightly as the one round gold earring that dangled from his left ear.

"Jesus Christ," Roland said. "You've really done it, you crazy fuck."

"Hard times require hard solutions," Billy replied.

They climbed up to Roland's apartment. The rooms were decorated with Japanese art and bonsai plants. The air smelled of thick, sweet incense.

"It's like a shrine," Billy said. "It's going to be perfect." After a lunch of brown rice, avocados, sprouts, and ribs, Roland walked Billy up to the roof. Billy smiled as he surveyed the panorama of the Golden Gate, the Bay Bridge, and the mountains beyond. Roland stared at him and shook his head.

"You look like the leader of a third-rate heavy metal band just back from a tour of junior colleges in Ohio," he said.

"Better than Mr. Clean, scumbag," Billy replied.

They hugged again.

Dear Sara,

Well, here I am, though God knows why. Sometimes you just have to do what you have to do. (Is that a country and western song?) I made a good start on my Beatles text on my trip out here. I am more convinced than ever that there is a special message in the songs for me. It could be of monumental importance for humanity.

Wyatt, I hope you're making progress with your guitar work. Remember, John Lennon didn't drop out of school until he was 15.

Jason, I enclose photographs of two pumper tankers that I found in the in-flight magazine. One is a Harley and the other is an American La France. Keep active. You never know.

B.

At dinner that night, after much cheap California Zinfandel and some grass from Roland's stash, they talked about old times.

Roland seemed confident that Sara would return once Billy completed his work. "How long do you think it will take you?" he asked.

"No way of knowing," Billy said. "It's not like the clues are just lying on the surface. Just a minute," he said. "Listen to this." He got his tape recorder from the suitcase and played Roland the notes he had made on the plane.

"You see," he said, "it's all there. I mean even my name. But this is just the beginning. I haven't started on side two yet. The problem is that time is running out." He told Roland what John's guru had said. "The twentieth anniversary is less than three weeks away."

"What do you think?" Billy asked after he had finished explaining his theory.

"Sounds pretty fucking major to me," said Roland. "Uh, you plannin' to do the Bee Gees next?"

MARTY ASHER

Roland got his job at the Post Office when young, male labor was at a premium because of the Vietnam War. He had been disqualified from service when he had painted a target on his head. After the war ended, all his co-workers went back to real life to become doctors, lawyers, CPAs, film producers, and rock stars. Roland, however, found the Post Office perfectly conducive to his mode of life. The hours were flexible, the benefits good. You could take off almost whenever you wanted. You could work stoned most of the time and either met interesting people or were stoned enough so that dull people seemed interesting.

Roland had already left for work when Billy woke up the next morning. He strapped on his Walkman, grabbed his tape recorder, and set out for a walk in the cool San Francisco sunshine. The clang of the cable car bells and the sight of the bay, spread out like dessert at the end of every street, filled Billy with optimism. The fact that this was the city from which universal visions of peace and brotherhood swept across the country pleased him. Surely a race that built this beautiful city was destined to survive.

But maybe only if Billy completed his appointed task.

Dear Sara, Jason, and Wyatt,

I have been in direct communication with John Lennon or a close representative of his. He seems to attach great importance to what I'm doing, though I'm not exactly sure why. Jason: John Lennon was a man who sang with Paul McCartney before he teamed up with Michael Jackson. You would have liked him.

I continue to make progress although this task is much more arduous than I ever imagined it would be. The music is so rich, and we've forgotten so much already. One can only try to approach it with purity and openness—as it was written—and not overlay it with the negative values one has subsequently acquired. I hope the restaurant is going well. I think of your zucchini fondly and trust I will be enjoying it again soon.

B.

One night at Ernie's, a popular North Beach coffee house, Billy told Roland that he believed John Lennon's murder was the Sarajevo of World War III. Probably no other single act could have demoralized as many people and convinced them that resistance to whatever was to come was futile. Billy was amazed that nobody had found or even tried to pursue a KGB or CIA connection. But maybe by the time the Lennon murder took place, people just didn't care enough or have the energy left to protest.

"Rock 'n' rollers," said Roland, after listening to Billy's hypothesis, "will not go down in history for the astuteness of their political connections."

Sitting on a bench in Union Square Park, Billy observed a small gray-haired man in a sea of pigeons, while a beautiful white one actually landed on his arm, walked up his neck, and pecked him on the cheek. Billy switched on the Walkman.

There it was again. . . . *With our love we could save the world.* Amazing. It was like they were following him to show him the way. I hear you, George. I hear you.

Was this song about drugs? Or something more? Billy remembered the disappointment he felt when he found his friends were getting stoned on acid and then watching "The Man from U.N.C.L.E." or some other idiotic TV show. Why weren't these people out proselytizing? Why weren't we a race of buddhas? What had gone wrong? Where had *Sgt. Pepper* failed?

On Roland's first day off, the two of them rented a car and drove to Muir Woods. Billy was in a dark mood and didn't want to talk much. "What's the problem, sport?" Roland finally asked.

"It's Sara," said Billy. "I miss her."

"Time to go home?"

"Sure, man," Billy snapped. "Sure I can go home and write my bumper stickers and count my money and live in my house like everybody else until the world blows up. It's not like you give a flying fuck about any of this. Just what the fuck are you planning to do about it?"

"Nothing meaner than a strung-out freak with a mission," said Roland.

Roland dropped Billy at the house, then went to listen to some jazz in North Beach. Billy slipped on his headphones, stuck his recorder in his back pocket, and headed for Chinatown. "Will you still need me when I'm sixty-four, sixty-four, sixty-four?" he sang as he sidled up to the lunch counter of a small cafe on Stockton Street. Why sixty-four? Why not sixty-five? "I was born in 1946," he whispered into his recorder. "Sixty-four is the reverse of forty-six. Someone born in forty-six will save the world in eighty-seven." He scribbled in his napkin: $87 - 64 = 23$. Twenty-three days from today would be January 1 or 1-1-87. $1 + 1 + 87 = 89$ or 8-9. August 9 was Billy's birthday.

"Keep talkin'," he whispered into the machine as he walked back home. "I'm listenin', John baby. I'm listenin'."

Late that night, John came again. Billy sat up in bed and saw him sitting on the window sill, legs stretched out, wearing faded jeans and a Rolling Stones T-shirt, hair short, gold-rimmed granny glasses tight against his face. He rapped blues beats against the window with a pair of drumsticks. "How's it going?" he asked.

Billy, exhausted after hours of playing, tracking, re-tracking, analyzing letter combinations and puns, and looking through foreign dictionaries, stared blankly at John and said, "Slowly, man. If the future of the world depends on my getting this, then head for the shelters."

John laughed. "Just keep working. You're on the right track."

"I am? I really am?" said Billy.

"You okay, man?" asked Roland, opening the door.

Billy looked to the window, but John was gone. "You just missed John," he said.

"And you just missed Lucinda," said Roland.

Billy now regarded the deterioration of the world more calmly. The trick was just to concentrate on one goal while blocking everything else out (something a lot of people apparently did every day). Negative realities could enter only if you let them. Certainly no missiles could possibly strike Billy while he listened to "Lovely Rita," and until he had finished his work.

Sitting on a bench at the Japanese Tea Garden, watching the water trickle down a mossy slope, Billy mumbled, "Rita meter, Rita meter, read a meter, read-a-me."

"I read you loud and clear, John," Billy said. "I just don't know what the fuck you're talking about."

Billy became a fixture at Union Square Park. He gradually came to know all of the winos, hustlers, bag ladies, and other San Francisco freaks. His favorite was a ten-year-old black shoe shine boy named Wiley, who seemed incapable of speaking a sentence without his voice slipping into a soprano squeak at the end. Though Billy had little money, he indulged himself with a dollar shine every morning.

"What you do here listenin' and writin' every morning?" Wiley asked one day.

"Just passin' the time," Billy replied.

"Yeah, but why you listen and write and listen and write and listen and write?"

"It's these songs, man. I love 'em a lot. So I just play 'em and write down what I think about 'em. You ever do that with Michael Jackson?"

"Shit, no," said Wiley. "I play the violin. I'm trying to get enough money here to go to music school. But what you gonna do with all that writin' when you finish it? It gonna be a book or somethin'?"

"Wiley," Billy finally said, "if you really want to know the truth, I don't think there's very much time left, and I'm tryin' to save the world."

"Don't bother me none," said Wiley. "Everybody in this park is tryin' to save the world. Wouldn't want people to meet the creator in dirty shoes."

MARTY ASHER

Billy cruised through Haight Ashbury, looking at the restored brownstones and quaint cafés that now lined its streets. He stopped in at one and asked for a coke.

"We don't serve coke," the waiter said. "It's full of sugar and artificial flavors. We have natural fruit-flavored soft drinks with carbonated spring water."

"Is this what it's come to?" Billy screamed. "You can't control the external environment anymore, so you focus on the internal? I mean is this the best you can do with your life, offering people organic cokes when you should be out there screaming to save the world? You keep this up your goddamned spring water's gonna be glowing in that bottle."

"Everyone takes care of their body," said the waiter, "their body takes care of their mind. Their mind takes care of the environment. The environment takes care of itself. Gotta start somewhere."

"We don't have that luxury anymore. It's too late," Billy retorted.

"You're from New York, aren't you?" said the waiter.

Billy grabbed a cab and headed for City Lights.

"I'm lookin' for books about Lennon," he told the clerk. She pointed him downstairs. He returned a minute later. "No, not the goddamned Russian, I mean John."

"John?"

"John Lennon. You know—The Beatles and all that. Maybe it was before your time."

The girl smiled. "Julian's dad," she said. "Music History, over on the left."

MARTY ASHER

Billy was asleep at the kitchen table the next morning when Roland staggered in. The table was littered with papers, album covers, liner notes, ashtrays filled with roaches, and the books about The Beatles Billy had managed to find. Roland made some coffee, looked in vain for a place to put his cup down, then just leaned against the wall.

"Good morning," he said. "You look like you've had quite a night."

Billy rubbed his eyes. He put his finger over his lips, popped the cassette out of his Walkman, walked to Roland's stereo in the living room and popped the cassette in. "GOOD MORN-ING, GOOD MORNING, GOOD MORNING," came roaring out at ear-shattering volume. Roland raced over and turned it down.

"You out of your mind, man? Can't you turn off for one goddamned minute?"

"Listen," said Billy. "You just came down here and said, 'Good morning.' What track am I working on now? 'Good Morning.' 'When I'm sixty-four turns out to be a numerical anagram for my birthday. 'Lovely Rita meter maid' sounds exactly like 'read-a-me,' get it? So I got all these books. Don't tell me it's a coincidence. There are just too many, and they're all here, man. I've got one day and two songs left, and the whole fucking world is waiting. Do you think I wanted this? You think this is easy?"

"When's the last time you ate?" Roland asked.

"Ate?" Billy repeated. "I don't know. Last night or the night before I was in a Chinese restaurant, so I must have eaten. What's the difference?"

"The difference is that I'd rather burn fast than slowly suffocate under a mountain of bullshit before breakfast."

"You don't get it," Billy laughed. "You just don't get it." He stormed out the door.

"We're not smart, but we're good hunters," Roland shouted behind him.

Looking down at North Beach and Chinatown, the Bay Bridge, and the lights on the hills starting to stand out in the clear twilight, Billy switched on his favorite part of *Sgt. Pepper*—the fabulous reprise. He listened attentively to Ringo's eight-beat introduction and smiled as the guitars entered. "Bomp bom bompbomp bom bomp bomp bompbomp bomp bya bya bya bya bya bya bya bya bya," Billy sang. As the first fog touched the towers of the bridge, Billy heard the words, *It's getting very near the end.*

"So it is," he muttered, and started walking fast.

MARTY ASHER

When Roland came home from work at midnight, he saw
Billy's gray metal emergency box on the kitchen table, open and
empty. Taped to it was a note:

Good Day Sunshine:
A Day in the Life Starts or Ends Tonight.
Hard Questions Require Simple Solutions.
   (That's a bumper sticker.)

And in the End, the love you take
is equal to the love you make.

Gone Fishing,
Billy

It was raining when Billy stepped outside, his Beatles notes in a black plastic garbage bag slung over his shoulder. He flicked on "A Day in the Life," took a deep breath, and felt his nostrils tingle with the electric burnt wood essence of San Francisco, one of the great smelling cities of the world.

Oh, boy.

John, wearing his chartreuse Sergeant Pepper uniform, stood on the beach, gazing toward Alcatraz.

"I'd love to turn you on," Billy said and threw his arms around him like the long lost friend he was.

"So you've got it," John said.

"It's right here," said Billy, patting his bag.

"It took you long enough."

"We still have an hour, don't we?"

"Yeah, but you've got to dig. Dig?"

Billy laughed. "Yeah, I dig."

"No," John said. "Dig. Dig?" John handed him a shovel.

Billy dug.

The rain sprayed off the bay in cold, hard drops.

When Billy looked up, John was nude, looking much as he did on the cover of the first album with Yoko.

"Put your manuscript in the hole," he commanded.

Billy obeyed.

"I want you to recite the words to 'Lucy in the Sky with Diamonds' backward and walk around the hole seven times clockwise and seven times counterclockwise."

"Oh no!" Roland screamed from a bench at the top of the beach. "Seven times counterclockwise and seven times counterwise!"

"What are you doing here?" shouted Billy.

"Great pick-up spot for white fisherladies," said Roland.

John got into the hole with the manuscript, started flinging the pages into the wind and screamed at Billy, "Now fix the hole! Fill it in!"

"But you're inside it."

"But I'm dead. It doesn't matter."

"But the music."

"That's dead, too."

Billy bolted.

Waist high in the freezing, slightly putrescent water, Billy heard a voice issue from the region behind his left ear that said, "People this stoned should not be waist deep in the water at this hour of the night alone. An objective observer might even think an attempt was going to be made here to turn off the pain by merging with this omniscient ooze, which is already a blend of so many different life forms and wouldn't care one way or the other if this human consciousness were added to the stew any more than if a clam decided to take a piss now if clams piss. You play the game and you play the music, but sometimes the game gets to be too much and maybe this is ultimately the only way to skip that other party with all those candles that no one ain't ever gonna blow out." But as the water reached shoulder level there came a loud splash and, wouldn't you know it, there stood John *on the fucking water* in a pure white robe, hair down to his shoulders looking so Christ-like and so loving and taking Billy's face and embracing it with those warm knowing hands, and maybe the body is just yanked out of the water or maybe it just thinks twice (it's all right), but there's no denying that voice soothing in the everloving Lennon tremolo, "Not yet, Sport, not yet," and Billy faintly offers, "What the fuck more can I do?" and then Roland, who has suddenly reappeared as well says, "You're going back to New York City; I do believe you've had enough."

"New York City. But of course."

IV

The door opened and John walked in dressed in his satin Sergeant Pepper uniform.

"I need some vitamins fast," said Billy.

Roland dumped them on the table and handed Billy a rum chaser.

"You almost joined me a while back there," said John.

"Maybe that wouldn't have been so bad."

"No, no, no, no, no," John declared. "Suicide is a highly unsatisfactory answer to life's problems. Besides, there are too many others depending on you."

"Why me?" asked Billy.

"Who else?" said John.

"How about you?"

"I'm dead."

"But if you're dead, how can you do it?"

"With a little help from my friends."

MARTY ASHER

Billy went to sleep and woke up.

"But where do I fit in?" he asked.

"You've got to make it happen, Sport. It's what you want and it's what we want."

Roland and John put their arms around Billy.

"What about my Beatles paper? Was that just an exercise?"

"We just wanted to warm you up. Make sure you are in the mood when the fun begins in earnest."

"And when does all this happen?"

"The plane is waiting."

Making the arrangements was not nearly as difficult as Billy had fantasized. The City Parks Department shared Billy's concern about annihilation (shit, nuclear war is not good for trees either) and helped Billy cut through the bureaucracy quietly and effectively.

The media, which Billy thought would just scoff, treated the event in a friendly way. A cover story appeared in *New York* magazine that was somewhat skeptical and viewed the event as a retreat from reality. "But," as Billy said at his press conference, "where has reality gotten us anyway?"

It was an extraordinarily beautiful sunny August afternoon,
with temperatures in the low seventies and a stiff northwesterly
breeze. Billy gasped as he looked out over the sea of bodies that
filled the Sheep Meadow. They spilled onto Fifth Avenue and
Central Park West. They climbed the rocks, the trees, and the
clock in Central Park Zoo. Thousands of balloons waved in the
cloudless sky. The pungence of marijuana exalted his nostrils.
Billy popped a few B₆'s and walked onstage. The crowd roared
when they saw Billy. He wore a blue jeans jacket and a JOHN
LIVES *button. He walked between the mountains of speakers*
slowly to the mike, still amazed by the awesome power of this
crowd.
"Hey, we did something today," he began.
The crowd roared its approval.
"The New York City Police Department (cheers) tells me that
there are over 4 million people here. That's the largest crowd
ever. Anytime. Anywhere in history."
Another roar.
"And we're here for one reason. We're gonna end the madness,
and we're gonna end it now. Now, I know a lot of you are
thinking just like I was. 'What the hell can I do? I'm just one
person, and it's just a matter of time before th maniacs in charge
of everything blow us all up. I may as well have a good time for
a while.'"
                    (BOOS)
"Well that just ain't good enough."
Billy was getting carried along by the crowd.
"Is it?"
"NO"
"IS IT?"
"NOOOOOO!"
"WHAT DO WE WANT?"
"PEACE!"
"WHEN DO WE WANT IT?"
"NOW!"

SHELTER

"IS THIS THE GENERATION THAT SHOWED WHAT MUSIC AND GOOD VIBES COULD DO AT WOODSTOCK?"

"YEAH!"

"IS THIS THE GENERATION THAT'S GOING TO OBLITERATE THE THREAT OF NUCLEAR WAR?"

"YEAH!"

"CAN WE DO IT?"

"YEAH!"

"I CAN'T HEAR YOU!"

"YEAH!"

"I WANT JOHN TO HEAR YOU!"

"YEAHHHHHHH!"

"Now you know we're not talking about going home and painting the barn. This is major and tough and boring shit. It's easier to get stoned, space out, and listen to Thriller."

(BOOS, CATCALLS)

"But we tried that. We tried dropping out, not worrying, getting our MBA's, raising our kids, and leaving government to those who know better, and look where we are. But that's all over, isn't it?"

"YEAH!"

"We're political now, aren't we?"

"YEAH!"

"I CAN'T HEAR YOU!"

"YEAH!"

"I STILL CAN'T HEAR YOU!"

"YEAHHHH!"

"You know why John is here today? Because he's concerned. And if he's concerned enough to make a spiritual journey to see us today, then are we concerned enough to write some letters and march on Washington or Moscow or whatever?"

"YEAH!"

"WHAT DO WE WANT?"

"PEACE!"

"WHEN DO WE WANT IT?"

MARTY ASHER

"NOW!"

"Now I think the boys are just about ready to give you the greatest concert of your life. Ladies and gentlemen, The Beatles!" And there they were. All of them. When they saw John in his granny glasses and jeans jacket, the crowd went completely berserk. Jason, Wyatt, and Sara, standing in the wings, jumped up and down and hugged each other.

"I DON'T BELIEVE IT!" people in the crowd screamed. "I DON'T FUCKING BELIEVE IT!"

The boys started off with "A Hard Day's Night," then slid into "With a Little Help from My Friends." They focused mostly on Sgt. Pepper and Rubber Soul, but threw in a few early classics like "Can't Buy Me Love" and "She Loves You." The concert went on for over five hours, and the last song was "Hey, Jude"— 4 million people, arms linked, singing, "Nannannannannanana," for over an hour.

Then, after the concert, came "The Announcement." With tears in his eyes, Billy said, "We've just received word that in light of the overwhelming turnout here today and at a similar concert in the Soviet Union, American and Russian leaders have agreed to start complete bilateral disarmament talks immediately."

The crowd cheered its brains out.

Roland brought Billy home two weeks later, as soon as he was strong enough to travel.

"We did it, man. We really did it," he repeated every few minutes, shaking his head back and forth in gleeful disbelief.

"Yeah, you poor fucker, you did it," Roland said to the wing.

MARTY ASHER

They landed in New York at midnight. Sara was waiting.

"God, you look great," said Roland, kissing her.

"Keep your lusting black eyes off her," said Billy.

"You know we're just animals." Roland winked at Sara. "Those big black things of ours just have a mind of their own."

"You touch her and you carry that big black thing back in your nose," said Billy.

"Hey, man," said Roland. "I do believe I'm going back to the gentle folk of San Francisco. These New Yorkers are just too tough for my sensitive soul."

Roland sat in the front with Sara. The two caught up on old times while Billy snored peacefully, huddled in the back seat of Sara's VW. Roland told Sara that Billy seemed eager to return home.

"He packed up so fast he didn't even take his Beatles tapes."

"What are you going to do with them?" Sara asked.

"Who knows? I've been hearing so much of them, I've actually gotten to like a few. I mean maybe they really *were* on to something."

"Roland," said Sara.

"Just jivin'."

MARTY ASHER

Billy woke up after about an hour. While Sara and Roland talked, he took out his pad and wrote, in the glare of the passing lights:

SOMETIMES THE ONLY SOLUTION
IS TO FIND A NEW PROBLEM

They arrived before dawn. Roland collapsed on the couch and fell instantly asleep. Billy tiptoed through the house. He looked in first at Wyatt, who had redecorated his room with Billy Idol posters on one side and Culture Club on the other. Some undefined, barechested hulk shrouded in pink smoke, wearing blue leotards and brandishing a humongous stainless steel electric guitar, glared down from the ceiling.

"Great kid, but no taste," he said, bending down and kissing him on the cheek.

Jason popped up, instantly alert, when Billy walked in the room. Billy sat down on the bed and hugged him.

"You're back," Jason said.

"I'm back."

"Where'd you go?"

"California."

"Will you tell me more stories?"

Once there was a boy named Dorian who wanted the biggest balloon in the world. His father bought him a bright blue one, but Dorian said that wan't big enough. Then he got him a red one that was six feet high, but Dorian said, "It's still not big enough." Then he went out and got a bright yellow one that was so big that it couldn't fit in the house and people mistook it for the sun. Every day Dorian and his friends and even strangers would stop to admire it.

One day a small purple bird landed on the balloon and pecked it. The balloon exploded so hard that Dorian's house was completely demolished.

"Then what happened?" asked Jason.

"His father bought him a smaller balloon."

"It's great to be back," said Billy later, in bed.

"It's great to have you back," said Sara.

"I have so many things to tell you about."

"First things first."

They slept till just before dawn. Then Sara got up and fried some eggs. A loaf of her infamous zucchini bread sat on a board on the table. A terra cotta pot of peppermint tea nestled alongside it. Billy cut enormous slices, slathered them with Sara's homemade blueberry preserves and stuffed them in his mouth.

"Hungry?" Sara asked.

"Starved."

Afterward, they walked out on the deck. Sara threw herself against Billy and kissed him so hard that he lost his balance and had to lean against the wood fence where she continued to climb him like a snake. Across the pine trees, behind the house, the sky started to shoot up bright needles of pink and orange. Suddenly "Here Comes the Sun" came pouring through the kitchen speakers. Roland grinned mischievously through the deck door, then came out and stood next to them.

"Couldn't find any Miles," he said.